This book belongs to

....

....

....

....

This is a Bright Sparks Book.
First published 2000
Bright Sparks
Queen Street House,
4, Queen Street,
Bath, BA1 1HE, UK.
Copyright © Parragon 2000

Produced for Parragon Books by
Oyster Books Ltd, Unit 4, Kirklea Farm,
Badgworth, Somerset, BS26 2QH, UK

Illustrated by Andrew Geeson
Written by Marilyn Tolhurst

Printed in Italy

ISBN 1 84250 062 7

A SCARY ADVENTURE

Illustrated by Andrew Geeson

Bright ☆ Sparks

It was a sunny morning at Faraway Farm. Danny and Rosie were sitting on the grass.

"I'm bored," yawned Danny. "There's nothing to do. I want to have an adventure."

"I want to have one too," exclaimed Rosie. Then added, "But not too scary."

"It has to be a bit scary to be exciting," insisted Danny.

He whistled to Conker.

"Here boy!" he called. "We're off to the woods."

"Can I come too?" asked Rosie.

"No," replied Danny. "Adventures are just for big people and dogs."

On their way to the woods, Danny and Conker stopped to say hello to Archie who was happily munching grass in his field.

"Come on, Conker," said Danny. "Let's make a den. It will be our secret place where we can watch out for enemies."

Danny and Conker hid in the den and kept watch.
"Ssssh!" whispered Danny. "Someone's coming."
They sprang out. Conker barked and Danny shouted "Gotcha!"

"It's only me, silly," said Rosie. "I want to have an adventure too."

Danny thought for a moment.

"All right," he agreed. "If you bring some food and drink, you can come in the den."

Danny and Conker settled down to wait while Rosie ran back to the farm to see what she could get from Mum.

"It's a bit quiet, Conker," whispered Danny nervously. "Quite scary, really."

Suddenly, Conker sat up. The hair on Danny's neck stood on end. Rustle! Rustle!

A twig snapped and then the roof of the den began to shake.
"What's that noise?" whispered Danny. Conker began to bark.

"Let's get out of here, Conker!" yelled Danny. The two of them raced out of the den as fast as they could.

They ran through the trees and bumped straight into Rosie.

"What's the matter? Where are you going?" asked Rosie, picking herself up.

"There's a monster attacking the den!" gasped Danny. "It's enormous! It climbed on the roof and..."
Rosie started to giggle.

"What's so funny?" demanded Danny.

"It's only Archie," Rosie laughed, pointing.

"He's eaten a great big hole in the roof."

Danny looked around and began to laugh as well.
"Aah, Archie" Rosie sighed, "Did you want to join in
our adventure too?"

"Come on, Rosie," said Danny. "Let's fix the den.
But this time we'll leave a little window at the back so
that Archie doesn't have to eat the roof to join in!"